THE ADVENTURES OF TOM SAWYER

by MARK TWAIN

#2 The Best Fence Painter

Adapted by Catherine Nichols

Illustrated by Amy Bates

STERLING

New York / London
www.sterlingpublishing.com/kids

Library of Congress Cataloging-in-Publication Data Available

10 9 8 7

Published 2006 by Sterling Publishing Co., Inc.
387 Park Avenue South, New York, NY 10016
Originally published and © 2004 by Barnes and Noble, Inc.
Illustrations © 2004 by Amy Bates
Distributed in Canada by Sterling Publishing
^{c}/o Canadian Manda Group, 165 Dufferin Street
Toronto, Ontario, Canada M6K 3H6
Distributed in the United Kingdom by GMC Distribution Services
Castle Place, 166 High Street, Lewes, East Sussex, England BN7 1XU
Distributed in Australia by Capricorn Link (Australia) Pty. Ltd.
P.O. Box 704, Windsor, NSW 2756, Australia

Printed in China 4/10
All rights reserved

Sterling ISBN 13: 978 1-4027-3288-1
         ISBN 10: 1-4027-3288-0

For information about custom editions, special sales, premium and
corporate purchases, please contact Sterling Special Sales
Department at 800-805-5489 or specialsales@sterlingpub.com.

Contents

Too Much Work

It was Saturday.

The sun was shining.

What a wonderful day

Tom Sawyer had planned!

He was going fishing

down by the river.

He got his fishing pole.

"Not so fast!" said Aunt Polly.

Tom's aunt had a bucket of paint.

She also had some brushes.

"Are you painting?" asked Tom.

"No, Tom," Aunt Polly said.
"*You* are going to paint.
You are going to paint
the fence outside.
Then you may go fishing."

Tom walked over to the fence.

How very long it was!

It seemed to go on and on.

He felt tired just looking at it.

Tom dipped a brush
into the white paint.
He painted for a bit.
His work looked good!

Then Tom looked at all
he still had to do.

"I will never finish!" he said.

How he wished he didn't
have to paint the fence!

How he wished to go fishing!

Then Tom saw his friend
Ben Rogers down the street.
Suddenly, Tom had an idea.
He knew a way to paint the fence
without doing any of the work!

Tom's Plan

Tom started painting again.
As he worked, he hummed.
Ben walked up to Tom.
  "Hello, Tom," Ben said.
"Too bad you have to work,
and on a Saturday, too."
Ben did *not* sound sorry.

Ben took a bite of his apple.

Tom's mouth watered.

How he wanted that apple!

"I'm going fishing," Ben said.

"I guess you can't come.

Not with all that work to do!"

"Work?" Tom said. "*Work?*"
"*This* isn't work to me!
I can fish any old time,
but I don't get to paint
every day, do I?"

Ben watched Tom paint.

It did look like fun.

"*I* want to paint!" Ben said.

"I don't know . . ." said Tom.

"You can have an apple," Ben said.

"Well, okay," said Tom.

Tom sat under a tree.
He ate the tasty apple.
He watched as Ben
did his chore for him.
His plan was working!

The Sweet Life

After Tom finished the apple,
his friend Billy Fisher came by.
Billy saw Ben painting,
and Billy's jaw dropped.
   "That is *Tom's* fence!" Billy said.
"Why are *you* painting it, Ben?"

"I want to," Ben said,
"and Tom is letting me
because *I'm* his friend."

Billy went over to Tom.

"*I* want to paint, too," said Billy.

"I don't know . . ." Tom said.

"You can have my lollipop," said Billy.

He gave it to Tom.

Tom gave Billy a brush.

Then more of Tom's
friends passed by.
Each one wanted
to paint the fence.
Tom let all the boys
have a turn . . . as long as
they gave him a treat.

Soon Tom was stuffed with goodies
and he had painted the fence
without doing any of the work.
He was the best fence painter ever!

All Done!

Tom could not wait
to tell Aunt Polly
he was done painting.
Now she would
let him go fishing!
Tom ran inside.

"May I go fishing?" Tom asked.

"So soon?" asked his aunt.

"How much of the fence
did you paint?"

"All of it," Tom said.

"*All* of it?" asked Aunt Polly.
"So soon, Tom Sawyer?
How could that be?"

"Come see!" Tom said.

Aunt Polly and Tom went outside.

"You did finish!" she said.

"I'm so pleased, Tom.
Come, I have a reward
for you, my dear."

Aunt Polly took out donuts.

"I baked these today," she said.

Tom took a big bite of one.

His tummy started to hurt.

He remembered all the sweets
he had already eaten.
He moaned and groaned.

"My tummy hurts!" he said.
So Aunt Polly quickly
sent him off to bed.

Tom saw his friends
outside his window.
They had fishing poles.
  "We're going fishing," Ben said.
"Do you want to come?"

Tom sure did,
but Aunt Polly said,
   "Sorry, boys.
Tom's tummy hurts.
He can't go fishing."

Then she gave Tom medicine.
Ugh! It tasted *awful*.

How Tom wished he had not
eaten so very many treats!
He promised himself next time
he *would* be the best fence painter—
one who didn't fool his friends—
one who painted his fence himself!